Corrie's Capers

The Tattoo Toorie

ILLUSTRATED BY
KIRSTY OXLEY

WRITTEN BY
ALISON PAGE

This book belongs to

....

For Sebastian

Other titles in the Corrie's Capers series:
The Westie Fest

You can find out more about Corrie on her website:
www.westie.scot

First published in Scotland in 2019

ISBN 9781999926519

Text copyright © Alison Page
Illustrations copyright © Kirsty Oxley

Corrie is dozing on her sitooterie enjoying the warm sunshine.
Oh, how she loves her cosy blanket and her comfy bed
overlooking Lamlash Bay.

DING
DONG!

Corrie runs to answer the door.

"Morning Corrie! Sorry to disturb your snooze time," barks Polly the Postie. "I have a special delivery for you. It needs to be signed for."

Mmm, I wonder who this could be from?

Very carefully, Corrie breaks open the seal and finds a card inside.

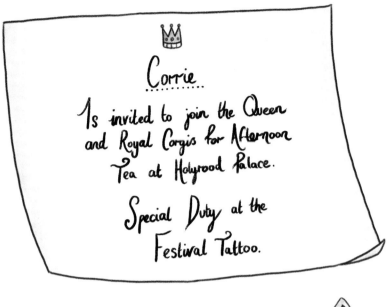

Corrie

Is invited to join the Queen and Royal Corgis for Afternoon Tea at Holyrood Palace.

Special Duty at the Festival Tattoo.

It's an invitation from
the Royal Family!
Corrie is to attend Edinburgh Castle
for the Festival Tattoo.

Woof-ity-woo-hoo! How exciting! And there's more…

At the close of the Tattoo, Corrie is to stand beside the Lone Piper and fire a single cannon shot. This will signal the start of the fireworks for the Festival finale.

What an honour! It's a splendid display which lights up the whole of Princes Street. The fireworks can be seen for miles!

Corrie's paws shake
and her knees begin to knock together.

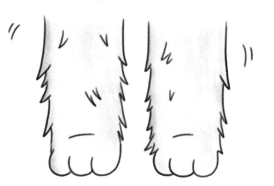

Her eyes well up with
big tear drops.

Oh dear,
what can the matter be?

It must be the fireworks!
Corrie gets so scared when they fizzle, crackle and bang.
She's not sure she's brave enough to fire that cannon.

But Corrie can't possibly turn down an invitation from
the Royal Family, can she? Dearie me, what will she do?

Corrie sets off to visit her Papa.
He always has helpful advice.

"Eeek!" Corrie cries. "What was that?"
Corrie's teeth are chattering and she's trembling all over.

Phew! It's just the exhaust from an old car struggling up the hill.

Corrie hurries on her way. She's desperate to ask her Papa what she should do about firing that cannon.

Gran Flora's Knit 'n' Natter group are packed into the cosy kitchen.
Their knitting needles click-clack busily as they chit-chat non-stop.

Corrie can smell Gran's freshly baked Woofibbles.

Yum, her favourite biscuits!

Papa always enjoys Corrie's visits, especially when the house is full of the "Knitting Nutters" as he jokingly calls them.

He sips his cup of hot sweet tea as Corrie pours out all her worries. "Mmm... U-huh... I see," Papa says, nodding his head.

Corrie munches her way through several biscuits
while Papa stares at the flickering fire, deep in thought.

Eventually he says, "Yep, I've got an idea which might work.
Let's go and speak to your Gran…"

The day of the Festival Tattoo arrives. Corrie was born in Edinburgh and loves spending time in "Auld Reekie", Scotland's capital city.

She enjoys a hippety-skip tour of Cammo and Cramond. She has wonderful memories of walking here as a puppy.

At lunchtime, Corrie heads up to Inverleith Park. Although it's a few miles away, there is a clear view of Edinburgh Castle.

Corrie checks the time and wonders if
she'll hear the One o'Clock Gun firing this far away.

Corrie hopes that her Papa's idea
will work when she's up close to
that cannon tonight.

After sharing Gran's Woofibbles with the Corgis at Holyrood Palace,
Corrie marches up the Royal Mile with the Arran Pipe Band.

The cobbled street is alive and buzzing with buskers and street acts all the way up to the Castle Esplanade.

The crowd hustle and bustle, jostling for the best viewing spot.

The Festival Tattoo is a spectacular event with pipe bands and dancers from all over the world. Corrie enjoys watching their perfectly practised performances so much, the time flies by and she almost forgets what she's there for!

Corrie takes her place beside the cannon poking through the castle wall. She reaches down searching for something in her backpack...

...and carefully places a beautifully knitted toorie on her head.

She stands beside the Lone Piper as he plays the lament.

It's Corrie's turn next.
Will she shake when the cannon fires?
Will she run away when the fireworks explode in the sky?

Gran and Papa are at home watching the Tattoo on the television.
They are sitting on the edge of their seats
hoping that their plan will work.

Corrie steps forward and lights the taper.

The cannon shot fires...

BANG!

FIZZZZ!

The whole sky lights up! What a fantastic Festival finale!

CRACK!

FWEEEE!

But why is Corrie no longer afraid of fireworks?

Her hat has ear plugs hidden inside it! The Knit 'n' Natter group are very clever at designing toories. Corrie cannot hear any loud bangs!

Papa boasts to everyone on Arran that Corrie has met the Queen AND fired the cannon used for the Edinburgh One o'Clock Gun.

He also asks Gran Flora to knit him a toorie just like Corrie's.
I wonder why?

Corrie and Papa are rascals…
The Knitting Nutters don't talk THAT much. Do they?

Follow the lines to discover which Toorie belongs to Corrie, Gran Flora and Papa.

 Did you spot any balls of wool hiding in the story?
How many are there?

Glossary

Sitooterie */sit-oot-eri/*   A place to sit outside under cover
Toorie */too-ri/*   A knitted hat with a pom-pom or tassel
Auld Reekie   A nickname for Edinburgh - "Old Smoky"

Alison's Acknowledgements

Dear John and Alexander,
Heartfelt thanks for your unconditional love and support.

With very special thanks to:

Kirsty Oxley for being a wonderfully gifted illustrator, so in tune with my requests for Corrie and her Capers.
Judith Paskin for being such a fab Editor! Timely, sensitive and an absolute professional.
June Caldwell for her kind patience and tip-top typography.
Richard Trewby for his time and keen eye.
Auntie Jeanie.bee and all members of Lamlash Knit & Natter Group who respond magnificently to all my Mary's Meals fundraising ventures. Nutters? Never!
Freya Campbell for baking yummy Woofibbles. These are Corrie's favourite treat and sell out very quickly in Brodick Post Office.
My dear friend Lynne Macvicar for her generosity and continuing support. In loving memory of a special Teddy Bear.

Find out more about Corrie's Capers at **www.westie.scot**
and Mary's Meals at **www.marysmeals.org**